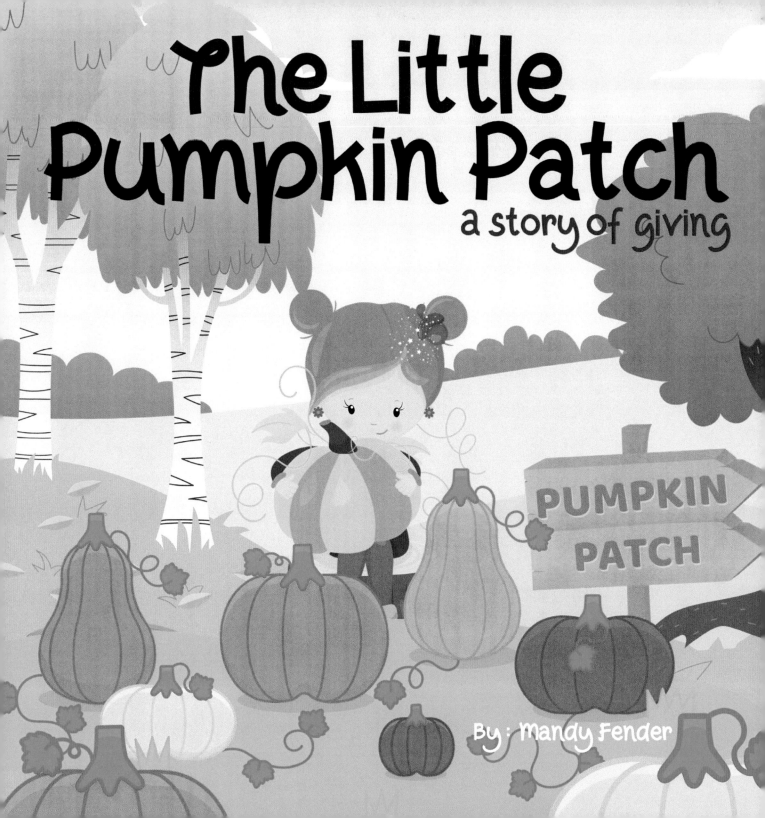

The Little Pumpkin Patch

a story of giving

By : Mandy Fender

This Book Belongs To:

Great Bible verses to go with the story :

it is more blessed to give than to receive.
ACTS 20 35 (NKJV)

So let's not get tired of doing what is good. at just the right time we will reap a harvest of blessing if we don't give up.
GALATIANS 6:9 (NLT)

The air turned crisp
and the season was changing.
"Goodbye, summer".
"Hello, fall!"
Piper squealed with delight,
It was her most favorite
season of them all!

The leaves were falling and turned all sorts of beautiful colors, especially orange, and that could only mean one thing…

The pumpkins in the little pumpkin patch that she and her family had worked so hard on planting were ready to harvest!

She had worked all summer long and all of her hard
work was about to pay off, and she would be able to
give pumpkins to each of her friends!

That night, she went to bed, knowing the next day would be the day all of her friends would see the little pumpkin patch .

Her sleep was sweet and filled with dreams of the most perfect pumpkins!
all of them different shapes and sizes, and special and unique, all in their own way, just like her friends,
who she could not wait to see!

The next morning, she waited outside, on her favorite swing, thinking about what a blessing it would be to give each one of her friends a pumpkin from the little pumpkin patch!

She was so excited, she shouted,
"Hooray, hooray! Today's the day!"

She thought long and hard about which
pumpkin she should give to each friend.

This tall one would be great for Tate because she's tall too!

This one would be great for Sally because she's quite silly!

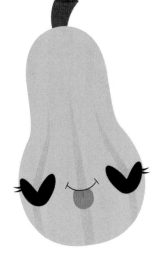

This one would be great for Molly because she's so lovely!

Piper worked very hard to get everything ready.

This pumpkin here.
That pumpkin there.

"Pumpkins, pumpkins everywhere!"
Piper exclaimed.

"Just as it should be!"

When her friends arrived to the little pumpkin patch, she could not wait to give them their surprises!

"I have a pumpkin for each of you!"
Piper said with great joy as she handed the
pumpkins to her friends with a smile on her
face.

Tate loved her tall pumpkin and would cherish it all season long!

Sally giggled and said hers reminded her of her goofy brother!

Molly hugged her pumpkin and thanked Piper a million times!

"What a wonderful way to spend the day!"
Piper said.

For the rest of the day, Piper and her friends
played in the pumpkin patch, went on hay
rides, and bobbed for apples.

all of Piper's hard work and patience had paid off!

She and her friends had the most fun fall day together with pumpkins everywhere, and it was on this day, Piper learned the joy of giving!

"Hip, Hip, Hooray!
What a wonderful fall day giving pumpkins away!"

The End

Thank you so much for taking the time to read *The Little Pumpkin Patch*! I pray that it was a blessing to your little ones and that it helps them remember that hard work pays off, and that there is great joy in giving!

Many blessings to you and your family this fall season!

Blessings,
Mandy Fender

Made in the USA
Middletown, DE
19 October 2022

13126712R00022